Flip the Flaps

Things That Go

Anita Ganeri and Mark Bergin

KINGFISHER

KINGFISHER

First published 2010 by Kingfisher
an imprint of Macmillan Children's Books
a division of Macmillan Publishers Limited
20 New Wharf Road, London N1 9RR
Basingstoke and Oxford
Associated companies throughout the world
www.panmacmillan.com

ISBN 978-0-7534-1922-9

1 3 5 7 9 8 6 4 2
1TR/0410/TOPLF/UNTD/140MA/C

A CIP catalogue record for this book is available from the British Library.

Printed in China

Contents

On the road   4

On the water   6

In the air   8

On the rails   10

On a building site   12

On the race track   14

Emergency!   16

Index   18

On the road

There are lots of different things that go on the road, including cars, trucks, buses and bikes. They have wheels to roll on, and most have engines to make them move.

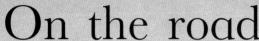

car

articulated truck

4

1. What makes a car go?

2. How does a bicycle slow down and stop?

3. Why do trucks have lots of wheels?

motorcycle

delivery van

bicycle

On the water

Ships and boats travel on the water. They carry people and cargo, or goods. They also do special jobs, such as fishing and rescuing people. Ships and boats are pushed along by engines, sails or oars.

submarine at the surface

raising
the sails

sailing boat

1. What makes a sailing boat move?

A container ship carries metal boxes full of cargo.

2. What sort of boat goes underwater?

A hovercraft carries passengers.

3. What sort of boat skims across the water?

A fishing boat has nets to catch fish.

In the air

Things that fly through the air are called aircraft. Most aircraft have wings that keep them up in the air. Many aircraft also have engines that push them along.

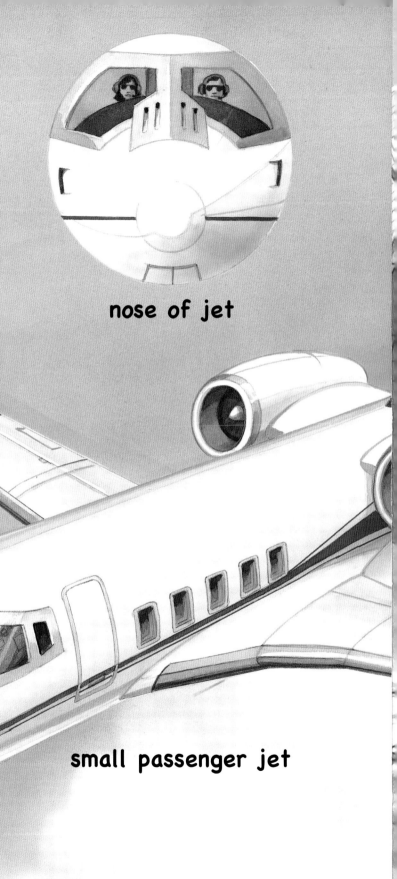

nose of jet

small passenger jet

8

1. How do an aeroplane's wings work?

2. Who flies a plane?

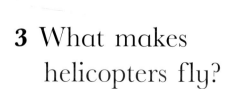

3 What makes helicopters fly?

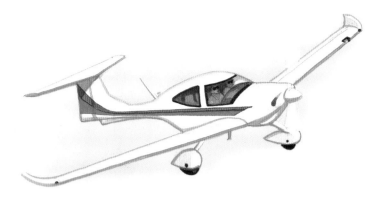

propeller plane

glider

helicopter

On the rails

Trains travel on railway tracks. Their wheels roll along on metal rails. Trains are very heavy, so they need a lot of power to make them go.

tunnel

passenger train

1. Do all trains have engines?

2. Can trains go underground?

3. Which trains go fastest?

A freight train carries cargo in wagons.

A mountain train climbs up steep slopes.

A high-speed train carries passengers, and sometimes cargo.

On a building site

Machines on building sites do lots of jobs. They help dig holes, move earth and rubble, and lift heavy loads. Big wheels or tracks stop them from sinking into the muddy ground.

crane lifting metal pipes

digger moving earth

12

1. What makes a digger's arm move?

2. Why do cranes need to be so tall?

3. How does a concrete mixer make concrete?

dump truck

bulldozer

concrete mixer

On the race track

Machines that go on a race track are fast! Racing cars have powerful engines for speed and wide tyres for gripping the track. It takes a lot of skill and practice to drive a car in a race.

racing car in the pit

crew putting on new tyres

14

1. How fast do racing cars go?

2. What gear do racing drivers wear?

3. How does a motorcycle go round bends?

saloon car

racing truck

racing motorcycle

15

Emergency!

Fire engines, ambulances and police cars are called emergency vehicles. They help people in danger or difficulty. Their loud sirens warn people to get out of the way so they can get to where they are needed.

1. A fire engine
   ladders that
   to climb into
   also has hose
   water on to

2. So that peop
   see them con
   let them go

3. A lifeboat w
   to rescue pec

1. What equipment does
   a fire engine carry?

2. Why do emergency
   vehicles have
   flashing lights?

3. Which emergency
   vehicle works at sea?

carries sick
ple to hospital.

takes police
mergencies.

elps people
at sea.

17

Index

A
aircraft 8
ambulances 16, 17

B
bicycles 4, 5
boats 6, 7
bulldozers 13
buses 4

C
cars 4, 5, 14,
   15, 16
concrete mixers 13
container ships 7
cranes 13

D
diggers 12, 13
dump trucks 13

E
emergency
   vehicles 16, 17

engines 4, 5, 6,
   8, 11, 14
express trains 11

F
fire engines 16, 17
freight trains 11

G
gliders 9

H
helicopters 9
hovercraft 7

L
lifeboats 17

M
motorcycles 5, 15

P
police cars 16, 17

R
racing cars 14, 15

S
ships 6, 7
submarines 6, 7

T
trains 10, 11
trucks 4, 5, 15
tunnels 11

U
underground
   trains 11

V
vans 5

W
wagons 11